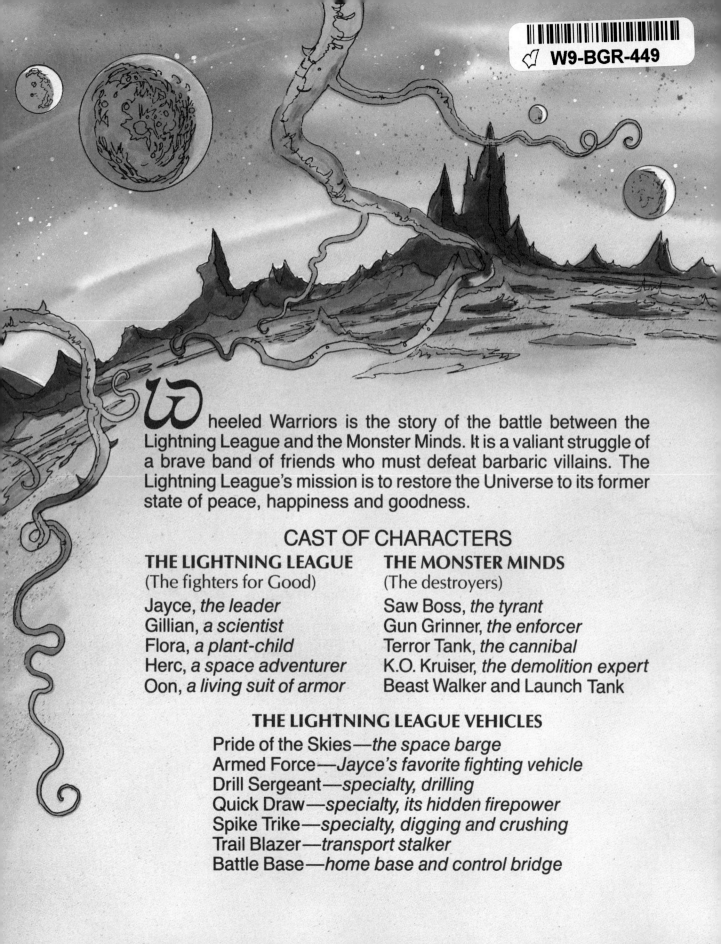

ⓦheeled Warriors is the story of the battle between the Lightning League and the Monster Minds. It is a valiant struggle of a brave band of friends who must defeat barbaric villains. The Lightning League's mission is to restore the Universe to its former state of peace, happiness and goodness.

CAST OF CHARACTERS

THE LIGHTNING LEAGUE
(The fighters for Good)

Jayce, *the leader*
Gillian, *a scientist*
Flora, *a plant-child*
Herc, *a space adventurer*
Oon, *a living suit of armor*

THE MONSTER MINDS
(The destroyers)

Saw Boss, *the tyrant*
Gun Grinner, *the enforcer*
Terror Tank, *the cannibal*
K.O. Kruiser, *the demolition expert*
Beast Walker and Launch Tank

THE LIGHTNING LEAGUE VEHICLES

Pride of the Skies—*the space barge*
Armed Force—*Jayce's favorite fighting vehicle*
Drill Sergeant—*specialty, drilling*
Quick Draw—*specialty, its hidden firepower*
Spike Trike—*specialty, digging and crushing*
Trail Blazer—*transport stalker*
Battle Base—*home base and control bridge*

WHEELED WARRIORS™

ROOTS OF FEAR

A GOLDEN BOOK
Western Publishing Company, Inc.
Racine, Wisconsin 53404

Library of Congress Catalog Card Number: 85-070079
ISBN 0-932631-14-2
A B C D E F G H I J

A call went out across the Monster Minds' planet. Saw Boss had sent the call to his three main warriors—Gun Grinner, K. O. Kruiser and Terror Tank.

The warriors wheeled toward the laboratory where they and Saw Boss had been created. The palace was now Saw Boss' throne room. Saw Boss, leader of the Monster Minds, did not like to be kept waiting. And so, the warriors hurried inside.

Inside the throne room, the Monster Minds were cut off from the dark energies that surrounded their world. Without those energies, the Monster Minds could not stay in their vehicular forms. They became ugly humanoid plant shapes and their weapons were almost useless.

"I never feel heroic like this," Gun Grinner complained. "I feel so out of uniform."

Without further complaint, Gun Grinner slid across the room toward Saw Boss' laboratory. Terror Tank and K.O. Kruiser went with him.

"We're here," said Terror Tank, "as you ordered!"

Saw Boss was busy with an experiment. "Come over here, I have something to show you—something very interesting."

"What's that?" asked K. O. Kruiser. He was the dull-witted warrior. "It looks like a seed."

Saw Boss smiled and held up the seed. "A very special seed that I have made," he said. "It will lead us to the defeat of our enemies—Jayce and the Lightning League."

Then, laughing with triumph, Saw Boss turned a strange ray on the seed. Instantly it began to grow.

Terror Tank, Gun Grinner and K. O. Kruiser moved in closer. Something was happening. The seed was growing fast. As it grew it began to change and soon it took on a shape that they all knew.

"It's turning into—a human!" exclaimed Gun Grinner.

"Keep watching," grinned Saw Boss.

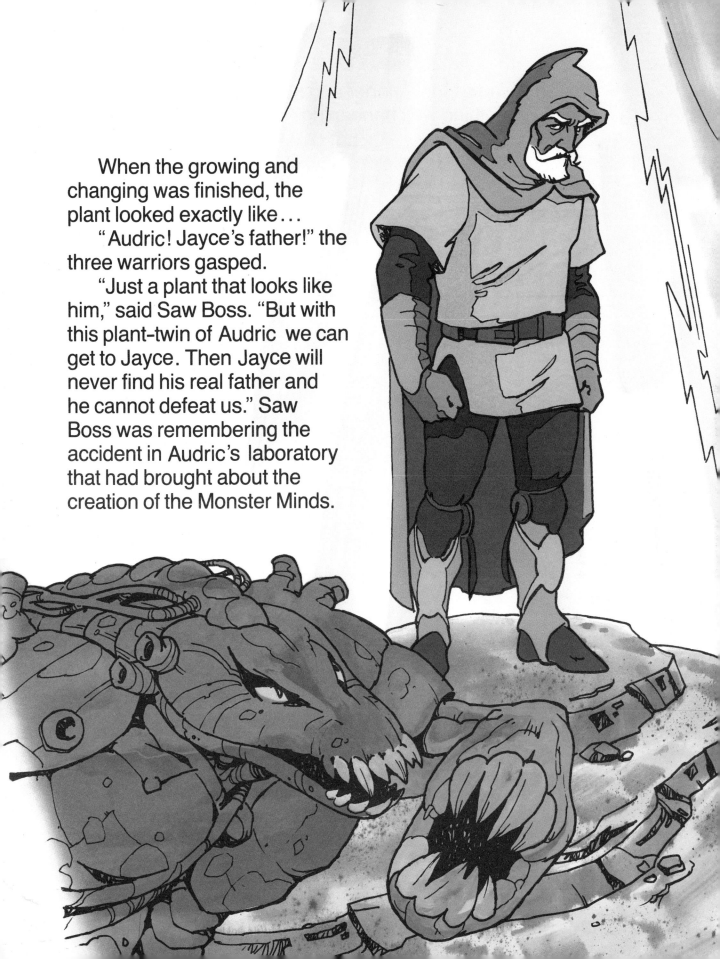

When the growing and changing was finished, the plant looked exactly like...

"Audric! Jayce's father!" the three warriors gasped.

"Just a plant that looks like him," said Saw Boss. "But with this plant-twin of Audric we can get to Jayce. Then Jayce will never find his real father and he cannot defeat us." Saw Boss was remembering the accident in Audric's laboratory that had brought about the creation of the Monster Minds.

Meanwhile, the Pride of the Skies, an old space barge, was speeding through outer space. Inside the barge, aboard the Battle Base, were Jayce and the Lightning League.

They were searching for Jayce's father.

"Ya'know, kid," said Herc Stormsailor, the barge's captain, "I don't think this quest is ever gonna end."

"We've been looking for your father so long that my ship's got space barnacles," Herc said. "And I still haven't been paid."

"I promise, you will be," said Gillian to the adventurer. Gillian was an ancient genius who had built the Battle Base and many other wonderful things.

Flora, the girl born from a flower in Gillian's garden, sensed Herc's thoughts. Herc wasn't as greedy as he liked his friends to think.

"We're grateful that you've helped us this long," Jayce began...but before he could finish his sentence, he heard radio static. With Gillian standing by, Jayce tried to contact whoever was sending a message.

A face appeared on the monitor screen. The face came into focus. It was instantly recognized.

"That's my father!" exclaimed Jayce.

The image on the screen did look like Audric. There was no mistaking his warm and fatherly smile.

"Jayce," said the monitor-screen image, "is that really you? Thank the stars! Then, I've found you at last! Son—you must come to me...alone. We must graft the plant roots that I developed. Then we can defeat those Monster Minds!"

"Where are you, Dad?" asked Jayce. "I'll come!"

'Audric' told Jayce where he was. Then the screen went blank.

"You heard my father," Jayce said to Herc excitedly. "Put the ship in that direction. I'm going to him!" For a moment Jayce felt more like a child than the leader of the Lightning League.

"It's hard to believe this has happened," said Gillian.

"It's great!" exclaimed Jayce. "Our quest could soon end!"

Jayce was excited about what had happened, for he truly believed it was his father on that screen.

"Have you changed direction?" he asked Herc.

"As you directed, kid. You're the boss," Herc replied.
"And we can't miss the planet we're headed for."

The planet was already looming ahead of the barge.

On that planet, the Monster Minds were getting ready
to greet the Lightning League.

A huge vehicle rolled over the planet's rough surface.
The machine was the Monster Minds' Launch Tank. It had
a huge mutated brain, and it thought for itself. Launch
Tank headed toward a big cave.

"That's where we'll spring our trap!" gloated Saw Boss.

Launch Tank opened its ramp. Out walked the plant that looked exactly like Audric. The plant-creature held something in its hand. It looked like the wonderful plant root that Audric had developed to save the universe.

"You know what to do," said Saw Boss from Launch Tank.

"Yes, master," replied 'Audric,' "when I hand this root to Jayce, he will be in for a big surprise."

"Good!" said Saw Boss, as Launch Tank rumbled away.

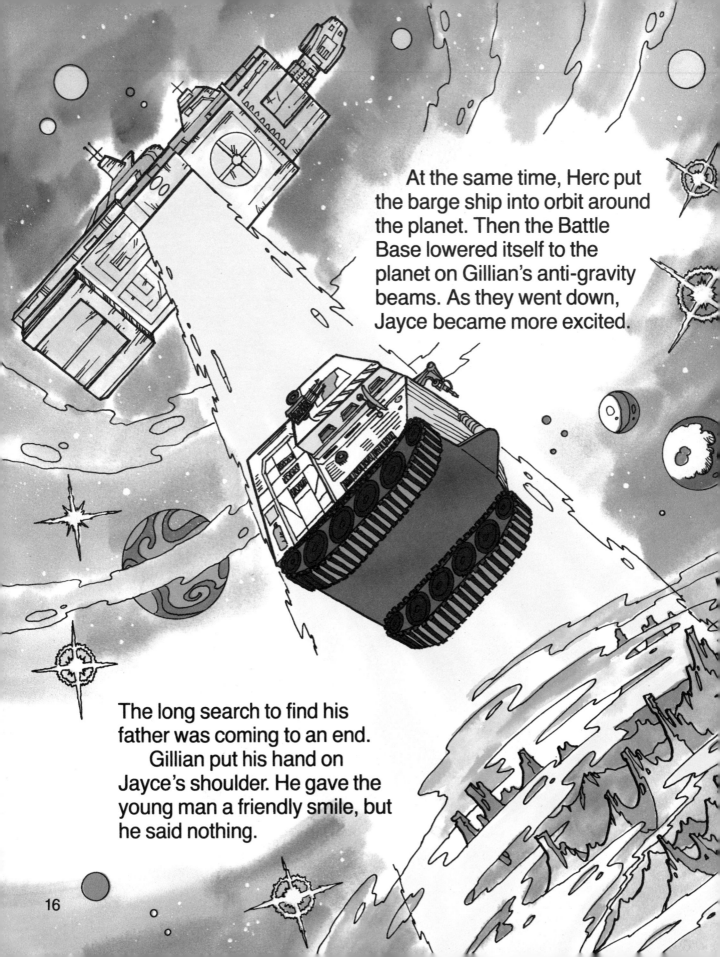

At the same time, Herc put the barge ship into orbit around the planet. Then the Battle Base lowered itself to the planet on Gillian's anti-gravity beams. As they went down, Jayce became more excited.

The long search to find his father was coming to an end. Gillian put his hand on Jayce's shoulder. He gave the young man a friendly smile, but he said nothing.

"Remember," said Jayce, "I must go alone."
"If you need help, just yell!" said Herc.
"Be careful," added Gillian.
Flora smiled at Jayce. Oon waved with his lance.
Then Jayce climbed aboard Armed Force. He started the
engine and the big machine headed off into the woods.

"I just wish he'd let us go along," said Herc.

"I know," said Gillian. "I have this strange feeling..."

"Maybe I can keep an eye on him," said Herc. He climbed into the telescope tower and turned it on. The tower rose from the top of the Battle Base. Herc looked through the telescope eyepiece and watched Jayce. "That's it ... keep in my sight where I can see you," said Herc.

18

Jayce followed the directions that 'Audric' had given to him. Along the way Jayce met many obstacles. Not wanting to lose a moment, he used Armed Force's grappling arm to clear the path ahead.

Soon, Jayce knew that his father was not too far away. He patted his jacket. The good plant root was still safely tucked away.

At last, Jayce saw a clearing in the woods. It was just as 'Audric' had described it. Behind the clearing was the entrance to the cave.

Jayce's eyes widened. Walking out of the cave was the figure of a man . . . a man that Jayce had known all of his life.

"Dad!" said Jayce, his heart beating faster.

"Son! . . . Jayce!" the figure said; the voice was familiar.

Jayce brought Armed Force to a fast stop. Then he jumped down and ran toward 'Audric.'

"Dad," he exclaimed, hugging the man he believed to be his father.

Jayce was so excited that he did not notice anything strange about 'Audric.' He did not sense the difference in the plant-like skin nor the coldness of the 'man' he greeted.

"We will have time to talk later," said 'Audric.' "But now there is something more important to think about."

He led the unsuspecting Jayce into the cave. "There it is," said 'Audric.' He pointed at something glowing with energy.

"Your hybrid plant root!" said Jayce. "That's the other half of your experiment that will save the universe."

"Quickly, Son," said the phony human being. "Where is your half of this wonder? I must graft the plants without delay."

Herc, meanwhile, became impatient. Too much time had gone by since Jayce moved out of the telescope's range. There was no longer any sign of him or Armed Force.

"Maybe I'm just an old mother hen," Herc told Flora over the tower's radio, "but I'm worried. I can't locate Jayce."

"Maybe Brock can help us," Flora replied.

Only Flora could understand Brock, the winged fish that had been created by Gillian. Her keen mind could translate his whistles. She told Brock what to do. He flapped his wings rapidly, then he flew away from the Battle Base.

Brock searched for signs of Jayce or his vehicle, but he found something else. It was not Armed Force, but one of the Monster Minds.

Flying as fast as he could, Brock returned to the Battle Base. He flew directly to Flora to whistle what he had seen.

"Oh, no!" gasped Flora. "It's the Monster Minds' Launch Tank!"

"Jayce is in trouble," Gillian said, getting more worried. "He should not have gone out alone."

"No use brooding, Gillian," said Herc. He rushed to Trail Blazer, the big Stalker. "Come along, Oon," he added as he grabbed Oon's armored wrist.

"Do you have to be so rough?" asked Oon. "I know you need me—a knight with a magic lance."

"I'm coming, too," said Flora, as she followed them. The engines roared, and Trail Blazer sped down the ramp on its rescue mission.

In the cave, Jayce was about to give 'Audric' the wonderful root that would save the universe.

"Ever since the exploding star turned my plants into the Monster Minds," said 'Audric,' "I've felt responsible. But now by grafting these roots, we can make *good* plants. And they will defeat the Monster Minds."

"Then," Jayce added, "there'll be peace in the universe."

Jayce held out the special plant root to 'Audric.' But instead of taking it from Jayce, 'Audric' made the two roots strike a glancing blow. Something awful happened. The cave filled with an explosion of light.

Jayce was stunned. The energies shocked him. He could not speak.

"You fool," laughed 'Audric,' "you let yourself be tricked!"

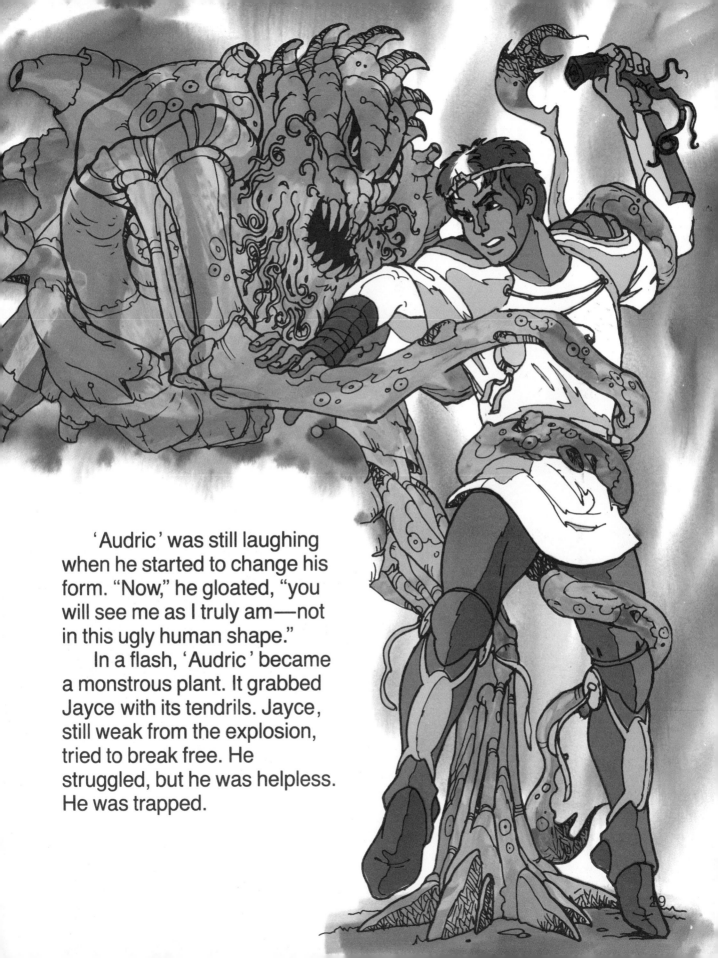

'Audric' was still laughing when he started to change his form. "Now," he gloated, "you will see me as I truly am—not in this ugly human shape."

In a flash, 'Audric' became a monstrous plant. It grabbed Jayce with its tendrils. Jayce, still weak from the explosion, tried to break free. He struggled, but he was helpless. He was trapped.

"Look!" roared Saw Boss. "The Lightning League's leader is wrapped up like a bug in a cocoon!"

Jayce could barely move, let alone get free. The weeds that had been 'Audric' were as strong as steel!

"Now that Jayce is our captive," said Saw Boss, "he'll never meet the real Audric. They'll never graft those plants. And we will be safe from our enemies forever!"

Jayce finally was able to speak. "You haven't won yet," he whispered.

"Don't flatter yourself," said Saw Boss. "You'll never break those vines."

The other Monster Minds laughed in agreement.

"Even if you could get free," said Saw Boss, "you'd need that precious plant-root your father gave to you. But I'll make sure you never see it again!" Saw Boss rolled toward Jayce and his treasure. Soon Saw Boss would claim it.

But Trail Blazer was on the move at top speed. Herc was driving the Stalker toward the cave.

"You're sure this is the place?" Herc asked Flora.

"Yes, and I'm getting brain waves from inside. I sense Monster Minds and I can also sense Jayce's thoughts."

"Okay, then! Hold on tight! 'Cause that's where we're going!" said Herc. He gunned the Stalker's engine.

Saw Boss moved closer and closer toward the hybrid root. He was enjoying the idea of owning the marvelous creation. Saw Boss was enjoying his victory so much that he did not hear the Stalker as it moved into the cave.

"Trail Blazer!" he said when he saw it. "We must stop it!"

The Monster Minds rolled to face the mighty machine.

"Save me the scraps!" said Terror Tank. "I'm hungry!"

33

All of the Monster Minds attacked Trail Blazer at once. Saw Boss zoomed forward with his buzz saw spinning. K. O. Kruiser swung the wrecking ball that he carried. It smashed everything in its way. Terror Tank snapped his fanged mouth at the Stalker.

"Oh, dear," sighed Oon, "we don't stand a chance against all four of them! We're doomed!"

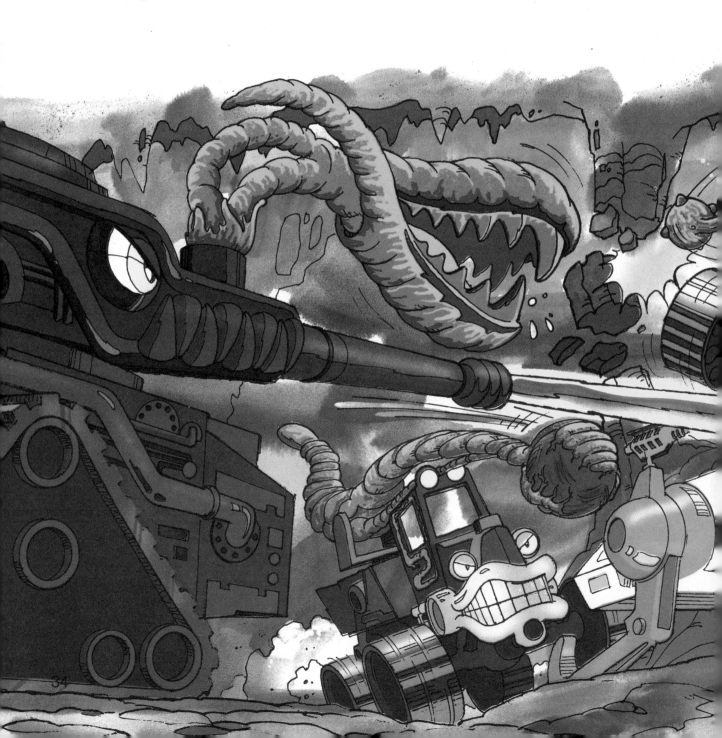

"I'll forget I heard that," said Herc. He steered Trail Blazer away from K.O. Kruiser's blow. The quick turn forced Saw Boss to dodge the same blow and his buzz saw hit rock.

"Hey, we fooled those two creeps!" bragged Herc.

"But what about the other two?" asked Oon.

Terror Tank and Gun Grinner rolled closer to Trail Blazer. Their guns sent powerful beams toward the Stalker.

Herc took aim. A second later, Trail Blazer's lasers hit some of the stalactites—the pointy rocks hanging from the cave's ceiling. The stalactites fell, crashing to the floor. The broken stones formed a huge barrier between Trail Blazer and the Monster Minds.

"That should hold them back," said Herc, "while I do what I gotta do!"

"You drive," Herc said to Flora. He slipped away from the Stalker's controls. "I'm going for a little walk."

"A w-walk?" said Oon, a little concerned.

Herc neared the place where he saw Jayce. To his disbelief, he did not see how Jayce could have bungled the job he had set out to do.

"We knew you were in trouble," Herc said, "but not this much trouble."

37

Flora defensively used Trail Blazer's weapons, as Herc hurried to reach Jayce. Inspired by Flora, Oon set down his lance and began to help her use the Stalker's weapons.

Herc tore at the weeds binding Jayce. "Use your strength, too, kid," he yelled. Together they broke the bonds. Jayce was free! The first thing he did was put the prized plant root back inside his jacket.

"C'mon," Herc said, "I'll race you back to Trail Blazer."

Rocks fell under Trail Blazer's energy beams. The cave roof began to split. Seeing what was happening, Flora and Oon stopped firing. Soon, the roof would fall down.

Saw Boss saw what was happening, too. "We must get out before we're trapped forever," he exclaimed. Buzz saw, wrecking ball and lasers attacked the stone walls of the cave. Terror Tank chomped on the iron-rich stone. Soon daylight began to show through.

While the Monster Minds escaped, Trail Blazer, with its passengers, roared out of the cave. Behind them came the rumblings of a cave-in. They had escaped just in time.

The Launch Tank was already leaving this planet on its space-vine highway. Again, the Monster Minds were defeated.

Finally Jayce had time to thank Herc for his rescue. "Thanks, pal," he said. Herc nodded.

When the barge was again traveling through space, Jayce said to his friends, "I acted in haste, but at least I did not lose the treasure that my father had entrusted with me."

"That's good" said Oon.

"And someday, I'll find my real father," Jayce said.

"You bet!" agreed Herc, and together the Lightning League spoke their motto: "'A Courageous Heart, A Righteous Quest!'"

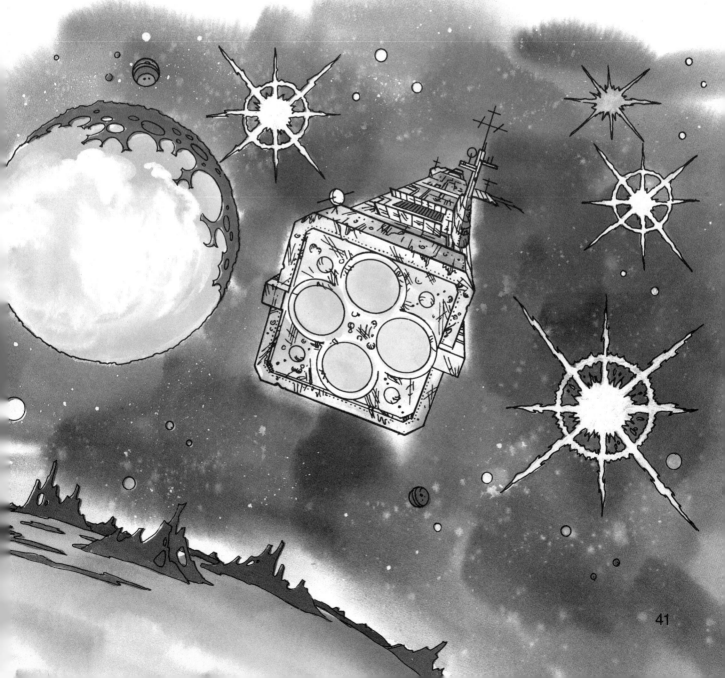